For Nora, my hoppy snow bunny
—Aunt April

For my parents,
who sent me to art school
and started it all,
and for creatures, large and small,
who run, skitter, fly, and crawl.
—J. U.

If You're Hoppy
Text copyright © 2011 by April Pulley Sayre. Illustrations copyright © 2011 by Jackie Urbanovic
All rights reserved. Printed in the U.S.A.
For information address HarperCollins Children's Books, a division of HarperCollins Publishers,
10 East 53rd Street, New York, NY 10022.
www.harpercollinschildrens.com

Watercolors on cold press watercolor paper with brush and ink outlines
were used to prepare the full-color art.
The text type is Billy Regular.

Library of Congress Cataloging-in-Publication Data
Sayre, April Pulley.
If you're hoppy / by April Pulley Sayre ; illustrated by Jackie Urbanovic.
p. cm.
"Greenwillow Books."
Summary: A rhyming text reminiscent of the traditional song "If you're happy and you know it"
presents various animals that are hoppy, sloppy, growly, flappy, or slimy scaly and mean.
ISBN 978-0-06-156634-9 (trade bdg.)
[1. Stories in rhyme. 2. Animals—Fiction.] I. Urbanovic, Jackie, ill. II. Title. III. Title: If you are hoppy.
PZ8.3.S2737If 2011   [E]—dc22   2010004103
11 12 13 LPR 10 9 8 7 6 5 4 3 2
First Edition
Greenwillow Books

IF YOU'RE HOPPY

BY
April Pulley Sayre

PICTURES BY
Jackie Urbanovic

GREENWILLOW BOOKS
An Imprint of HarperCollinsPublishers

IF you're hoppy

and you know it,

you're . . .

a frog.

A FROG!

If you're hoppy and you know it,
you're a frog.

OR . . .

A BUNNY!

If you're hoppy
and you know it,
stretch your toes to really show it.

If you're hoppy and you know it,
you're a frog.

Or a bunny.

Or a cricket!

Crick, crick!

If you're
SLOPPY
and you know it,
you're a hog.

A HOG!

If you're sloppy and you know it,
you're a hog.

OR . . . A RACCOON!

If you're sloppy and you know it,
squeeze your face to really show it.

If you're sloppy
and you know it,
you're a hog.
Or a raccoon.
Or a chimp.

OR . . .

A BABOON!

If you're GROWLY
and you know it, you're a dog.

A DOG!

If you're growly and you know it,
you're a dog.

OR . . .

A BEAR!

If you're growly and you know it,
make a sound to really show it.
If you're growly and you know it,
you're a dog.

Or a bear.

OR . . . A TUMMY, OVER THERE!

If you're FLAPPY
and you know it, you're a bird.

A BIRD!

If you're flappy and you know it,
you're a bird.

OR . . . A BUTTERFLY!

If you're flappy and you know it,
swing your wings to really show it.

If you're flappy and you know it,
you're a bird. Or a butterfly.

Caawk!

Caawk!

Or a
PTERODACTYL
in the sky!

If you're slimy and scaly
and mean, you're a . . .

oh, never mind.

If you're slimy and scaly and mean, you sound like . . .

oh, never mind.

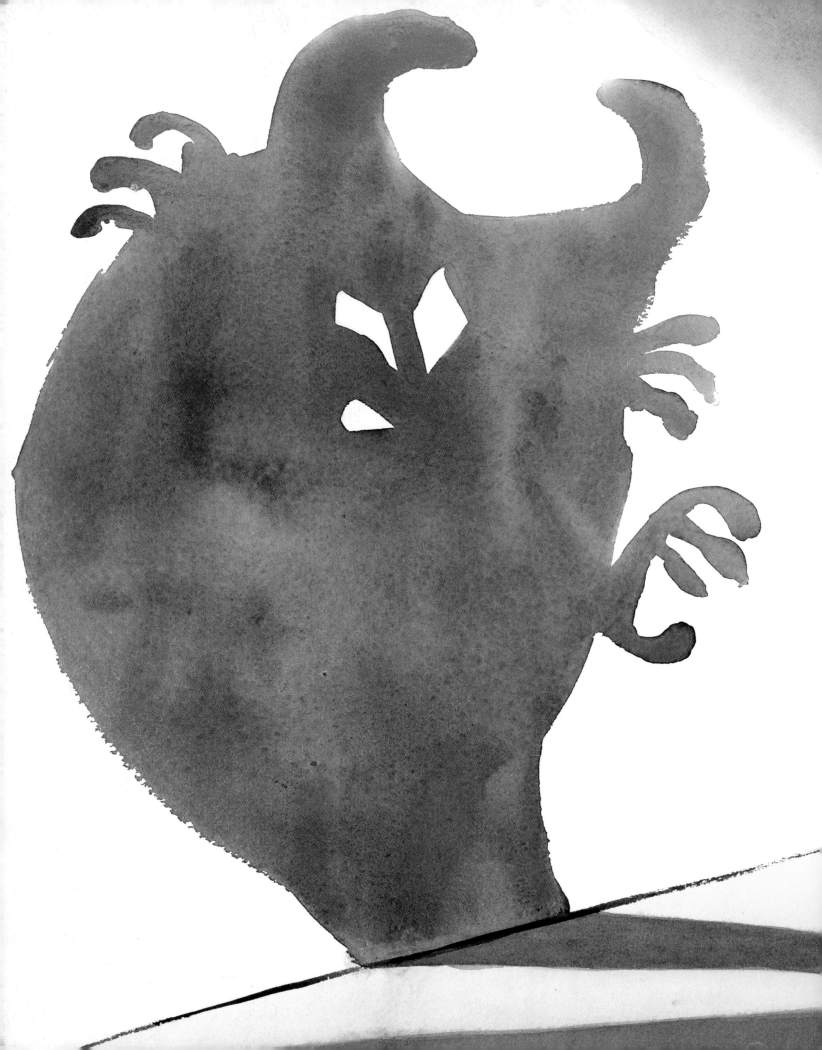

If you're slimy and scaly and mean,
perhaps you'd rather not be seen.
So if you're slimy

and scaly

and mean,

just never mind.

If you're
sloppy
and you know it,
you're

A HOG!

(Feel free to show it!)

If you're hoppy
and you know it,
you're a
frog.

A FROG!

I'm
so
happy
hopping . . .

hop,

hop,

hop

WITH YOU!

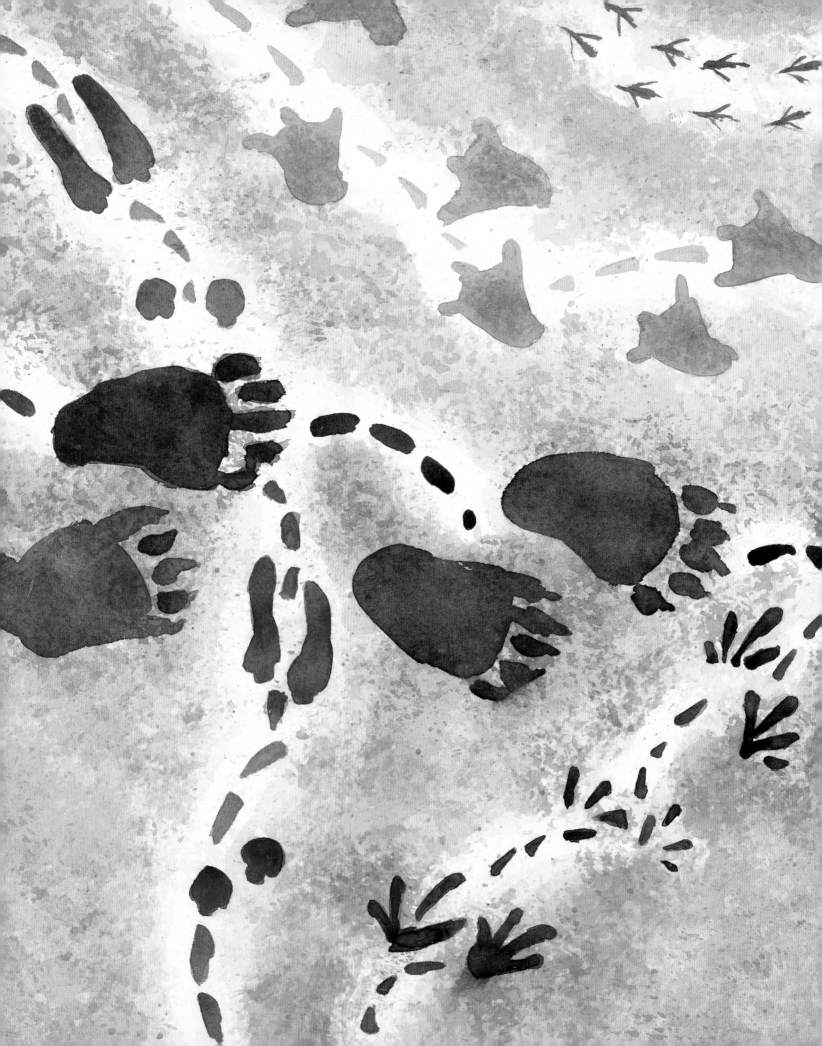